This book was produced with cooperation among:

Kariuki Gakuo, the author

Mwaura Ndekere, the artist
and the
Museum Hill Gallery,
Nairobi, Kenya

Dedication

"...For 'Mama' and all mothers
from whose hearts' spring a million stories."
K. G.

"...To my art teacher, L. Muriuki who opened my eyes
to the world of colour."
M. N.

Acknowledgements

Our acknowledgements and thanks are due Professor Godfrey Muriuki of the Department of History, University or Nairobi; Professor Karega wa Mutahi of the Department of Linguistics and African Languages, University of Nairobi; and Wanjiku Mukabi Kabira, Department of Literature, University of Nairobi, for their invaluable assistance in reading this manuscript and authenticating the material. Special thanks also go to the Kenya National Archives for the use of their materials and to the Art Director of Museum Hill Gallery, Eustace Gitonga, for his support and guidance.

Published by **Jacaranda Designs, Ltd.** P.O.Box 76691 Nairobi, Kenya
 First published 1992

ISBN 9966-884-72-6

Text by Kariuki Gakuo. Original paintings by Mwaura Ndekere.
Graphic Design by Ladan Doorandish-Vance. Edited by B. A. C. King
Typeset in Palatino. This product was produced and published entirely in Kenya.

Nyumba Ya Mumbi
The Gikuyu Creation Myth

Foreword

Every community has its share of oral literature which explains its origins. Many traditional stories tell us about ourselves and our past. Such narratives remind us of our beginnings and that our communities have a mother and a father.

Although these stories do not necessarily contain historical facts, they are never-the-less important because they provide insight into our beliefs, lifestyle and the foundations on which these are based.

From generation to generation, these stories have been handed down orally. Today, however, few of us have the chance to listen to their oral renditions due to our fast pace of change in modern society. It is therefore important that these narratives be recorded for the sake of posterity.

Nyumba ya Mumbi, has now been evocatively illustrated and creatively retold for future generations. It is a story about the genesis of the Gikuyu community, written with a beauty and skill to match the flavour which traditional storytellers bring to their performance. This rendition of *Nyumba ya Mumbi* pays tribute to our literary traditions!

When you have read it, ask your grandmother to tell you a story like this from your own community or another community. As the people of Kenya, we can learn about one another in this way for our heritage is rich! Let us cherish our inheritance and keep it alive!

Wanjiku Mukabi Kabira
Department of Literature
University of Nairobi

According to the oral traditions of the Agikuyu, the descendents of *Gikuyu* and *Mumbi*.......

In the fiery dawn of time,
when the earth trembled in the throes
of creation a dense cloud of mist
stood over the land,
as *Mugai,* the divider of the Universe
descended to earth,
to his seat of mystery.

There, upon the dazzling
snowcapped peaks of the black
crystal mountain called *Kirinyaga* [1],
he made a dwelling place.

From that day,
the mountain became his chief abode
and was revered as sacred ground.

According to Gikuyu legend,
Mugai led *Gikuyu,*
father of the Gikuyu nation,
to the misty peaks of the sacred mountain.
Pointing out the beauty
of the land lying below
he said:

"You shall carve your inheritance
from this land,
It shall belong to you
and your children's children
to be passed
from generation to generation
until the twilight of existence."

And so it became.
The Agikuyu were given
the land of rivers and ravines,
of hills and valleys,
of forests with all the
creatures therein,
and all the gifts of nature that
Mugai, divider of the Universe,
had bestowed on his people.

As the morning sun broke
through misty skies,
Gikuyu did as his creator
had commanded.
He descended to
Mukurwe wa Gathanga [2]
where a grove of
sacred fig trees grew
in rich red earth.

Resting in the shade
of the sacred grove,
he found the most
beautiful of women.
Taking her to be his wife,
he named her *Mumbi*,
the creator or moulder
of the tribe.

From the sacred *Mukuyu* grove,
Gikuyu took his name.
Together,
Gikuyu and *Mumbi* built a home
And gave birth to nine daughters[3]
Wanjiru, Wambui, Wanjiku,
Wangari, Waceera, Wairimu,
Wangui, Wangechi, Wambura
and *Wamuyu.*

The nine daughters of *Mumbi*
grew and became happy
and hardworking girls.
In the misty cool of dawn,
their gentle fingers
tilled the rich earth
and returned it to life.
Out of the earth came forth
all manner of crops, millet,
sugar cane, arum and yams,
and the family of *Mumbi*
prospered.

In the shimmering heat
of the midday sun,
the girls led their father's flocks
to watering holes ,
to drink from
crystal clear streams
that ran down the hills
and valleys.

In the evening, when the flocks
came home from grazing,
the sound of pounding pestles
filled the air.
The voices of the nine daughters,
rich with the melody
of grinding grain,
carried over the trees
and onto the plains.

After many moons had gone by,
the nine girls grew into beautiful women
who rippled with the beauty of the full moon.
Their eyes twinkled like stars in the moonlight,
while their breasts, full and ripe, stood proud
as the dazzling peaks of *Kirinyaga*.
Their enchanting laughter was like the sweet chorus of birds
and their milky teeth glittered like white doves in flight.
When they walked,
the melody of the beads around their waists
rose to the sky, deep, sombre and enchanting.

But with the passing of every full moon,
they felt the flow of the rising tide
searing like glowing firewood in their wombs.
They beseeched their parents:
"For many seasons you have held and comforted us
but we now wish to have homes of our own
so that your names may be
whispered from generation to generation."

For many moons, *Gikuyu* and *Mumbi* searched their hearts as they walked the breadth of the land.

At last, in despair, *Gikuyu* fell upon his knees. Raising his face to *Kirinyaga* he called upon *Murungu* [4], his creator, to bless his daughters with husbands. *Murungu* heard him and commanded *Gikuyu* to make a sacrifice at the foot of the sacred *Mugumo* tree.

In the centre of the land stood a tree, tall, firm and ancient like the passage of time. The sacred *Mugumo* tree. Here the spirit of *Ngai* [5] resided. No man was permitted to cut down or break any branch from this tree, nor to clear any of the bush around it. Any bird, animal or living creature which took sanctuary at the foot of the tree was safe in the hands of *Ngai*.

It was here that *Gikuyu* did as his creator had commanded. He brought a lamb, a kid and nine burning sticks, each stick being the length of his daughters' shadows. Sacrificing the lamb and the kid, *Gikuyu* sprinkled their blood and fat onto the trunk of the sacred tree.

At the foot of the tree *Gikuyu* lit a fire with the nine burning sticks, and as the fat crackled in the fire and the roaring flames rose into the sky, he called out unto *Murungu,* his creator, saying:

"We have come to beseech you for rain, which sustains our children, and our children's children. Say now that the rain may fall:

> Children *thaai uthaai*
> Rain *thaai uthaai*
> Cows *thaai uthaai*
> Goats *thaai uthaai*
> *Thaai thathaiya Ngai thaai.*" [6]

As *Gikuyu* continued to chant this invocation,
out of the fire came nine flaming young men
whose backs were firm and strong
Like the trunk of the *mugumo* tree,
yet as supple as the *mukengeria* [7] creeper.
When *Gikuyu* saw the nine men
he spat on his chest,
and lifting his arms in supplication
he gave thanks and praise to *Murungu*
for heeding his cry.

In his seat of mystery
Murungu lit up the sky with his flashing sword of fire
while his voice rumbled with thunder.
The pregnant clouds showered their blessings on the earth
and put out the fire.

The nine men were welcomed into *Gikuyu's* homestead
with greetings and ululations.
Gikuyu's daughters wept with joy
for now they could have many children
and be blessed among women.
A ram was killed for their evening meal
and while the millet gruel simmered over a wood fire
the men were taken to a nearby stream
to wash their tired limbs.

In the heart of the night,
when the stars twinkled like a thousand fireflies,
they told tales and sang around the fire.

The nine handsome, young men could not resist
the alluring beauty of *Mumbi's* daughters,
or the kindness and generosity of *Gikuyu's* homestead.
Early the next morning they asked
Gikuyu and *Mumbi* for their daughters' hands in marriage.

Gikuyu, father of the Agikuyu,
blessed the marriages.
Each daughter had her own hut and family.
The name of the house of *Mumbi* prospered,
its fame spreading throughout the hills and valleys,
within and beyond the land which *Mugai* had given them.

When *Gikuyu* and *Mumbi* passed away,
each daughter called together all her descendants
forming one clan under her own name.

In this way, the nine full *mbaris*, or clans, of the
Agikuyu were formed.
These nine clans merged together in unity,
kinship and solidarity.
This group was given the ancestral name of
Ruuriri rwa Mbari ya Mumbi
or as it is known today,
Nyumba ya Mumbi.

To this day,
when the Agikuyu call upon their creator,
they turn their faces to the top
of the snow clad mountain.
Raising their arms, they chant the sacred invocation:

"Thaai thathaiya Ngai thaai."

Endnotes:

1. ***Kirinyaga***: The mountain was called *Kirinyaga* because of the dazzling brightness of the snow as it glittered off the black crystal rock. From a distance this looks like black and white stripes. *Ngai,* the supreme ruler of the universe is also known as *Mwene Nyaga,* the owner of the stripes of *Kirinyaga.* The mountain is also known as *Kirimaara,* the spotted mountain.

2. ***Mukurwe wa Gathanga,*** or *Mukurwe wa Nyagathanga* is in the Gaturi location of Kiharu Division in Muranga District, about 20 kilometres west of Muranga town on the way to Kiriaini.

3. ***Gikuyu* and *Mumbi*** had ten daughters but according to Gikuyu custom children are not counted as this is regarded as a bad omen that may lead to death. The Agikuyu therefore speak of the "*Kenda Muiyuru*" or the nine full clans of the Agikuyu instead of calling them ten. Gikuyu's tenth daughter *Wamuyu,* who was also the youngest, became the mother of the *Aicakamuyu* clan. According to the legend, when Gikuyu told his daughters to bring him the ritual sticks, she failed to do so and therefore did not get a husband. It is said that she later bore children while still in her father's home and her children became the tenth clan of the Agikuyu.

4. ***Murungu***: In prayers, *Mugai,* the supreme deity, is referred to as *Murungu Mwenehinya.* This is the original name for God in most Bantu languages derived from the root *dungu.*

5. He is also referred to as *Ngai* - the one who distributes shares.

6. This is a ritual prayer, used when praying for rain. In Kikuyu the words *'Thaai thathaiya Ngai thaai'* mean "Praise be to God, May peace be with you."

7. ***Mukengeria:*** This is a creeping herb with bright blue flowers, jointed stems and fleshy roots. Its botanical name is <u>commelina benghalensis</u>. It is used as a fodder crop for fattening goats and sheep. Traditionally its leaves and stems were used in purification rites, while the leaves were also used in the ceremony of building a new hut after an old one had burnt down. Its juice was also used as an antiseptic during initiation ceremonies.

About the Author

Kariuki wa Gakuo was born in 1964 in Kirinyaga District.

A graduate of the University of Nairobi, he has done a Master's Degree in Oral Literature and enjoys writing poetry, fiction, drama and short stories. His writings have appeared in many newspapers and magazines including *Viva*, *New Age* and the *Daily Nation*.

When he is not writing, he enjoys playing music, travelling and acting on stage.

Kariuki is a fulltime writer with Jacaranda Designs, Ltd.

About the Artist

Mwaura Ndekere was born in Muranga District and is a graduate of Kenyatta University in Nairobi where he earned a Master's Degree in ceramics.

At twenty-nine, he has taken part in group exhibitions locally and in the Netherlands.

He is currently associated with Museum Hill Gallery where he exhibits a wide variety of works of art including paintings and ceramics. People and landscapes form the central themes in his art.

He is married with two children.

Bibliography

Leakey, L. S. B. The Southern Kikuyu before 1903 (Vol. 1-3)
London: Academic Press 1977

Kabetu, M. N. Kirira Kia Ugikuyu
Nairobi: East African Literature Bureau, 1966

Kenyatta, Jomo Facing Mount Kenya
London: Martin Secker and Warburg Ltd., 1938

Kenyatta, Jomo My People of Kikuyu
Nairobi: Oxford University Press, 1966

Muriuki, Godfrey A History of the Agikuyu 1500 - 1900
Nairobi: Oxford University Press, 1974

Wanjau, Gakaara Thooma Giigikuyu Kiega (Ibuku ria Gatatu)
Karatina: Gakaara Press, Ltd. 1986